Lüz

Lindsay Stern

Cover image: Leandro Katz, "Lunar Typewriter" (from The Lunar Alphabet project), Copyright ©1978.

ISBN: 978-0-9985463-1-5
LCCN: 2017933368

FIRST EDITION

Published by
Ravenna Press
ravennapress.com

Preface

Not long ago, I was clearing the snow off a frozen pond when I noticed a pattern in the ice. It was a web of some sort, vessels branching off one another and connecting in alabaster points. The more feverishly I swept—with the nose of a ski pole—the more complex it appeared. Only after I had cleared off a patch wide enough to stand on did I realize my oversight. What I had been trying to expose were fissures in the ice, wrought by my own efforts.

Sheepish as it made me feel, that experience of participant observation confronted me with a pair of questions that inspired the following document: Is inquiry a form of invention? If so, under what conditions, and how might invention—literature, in particular—constitute an act of inquiry? The two protagonists of this book navigate both questions, drawing in their pursuits on both dialectical and imaginative thought. Their dialogue unfolds over the course of one evening, interrupted by vignettes that chronicle the genesis and fall of the world they inhabit. As such, the narrative does not constitute a work of "fiction" in the traditional sense of the term. It is intended instead as an (perhaps failed) experiment in uniting two ancient and mutually hostile modes of understanding: argument and myth.

This project owes a special debt to the ideas of Luis Buñuel, Anne Carson, M.C. Escher, Sigmund Freud, Kurt Gödel and Plato; and to the lie detector of a certain professor of Philosophy at Amherst College. The detector, which he keeps on a file cabinet near the window, flashes either green or red in response to surrounding noise. (Woe to the student who, defending her request for an extension, earns a verdict of red.) On one particular afternoon, I walked in to find just such a verdict already flashing. The room was quiet. No one was speaking. The machine was picking up the melody of an apparently mendacious bird.

That incongruous appraisal sparked a second pair of questions to which this document responds. What would it mean to treat the natural world as a language? How, in their separate ways, do both science and religion do just that, and what—in so doing—do they presuppose about human understanding?

What follows, then, is part artifice and part inquiry into the project of knowing the world—that is, into the attempt to circumscribe reality, whether through analysis or invention. I set out to explore what motivates that attempt, its tragicomic limits, and how it might function as a response to guilt and loss. My questions yielded the following document, a portrait of a society united and estranged by its use of signs. I called that society "Lüz" for its double sense: both a homonym of "lose, v." and—minus the umlaut—the Spanish word for light.

Author's Note

All surviving records of Lüz and its inhabitants were discovered by the aforesaid on or before September 30, 2013. Consulted archeologists have confirmed that the primary sources [pp. 6, 73, and 75-6] share no single author. As such, they are best interpreted as cultural data—offshoots, as it were, of a collective mind.

"There is at least one sense in which the human is not alone in the world: her conviction otherwise."

- Unknown [Lüz, c. Year 23]

Lüz

1

From Years 1 to 48, the people of Lüz fell victim to the mistaken belief that the night sky spoke in pictures. "Constellations," they called them. An astronomer discovered the truth in Year 49, and published her results in the Daily Gazette. The night sky, it turned out, spoke in Braille:

"Love thy neighbor."

"Out to lunch."

"I am sorry you are cold."

By noon, the astronomer's petunias were bald. Half the population of Lüz had stampeded her garden. The other half had knocked a hollow in her door. Undaunted, the astronomer telephoned City Hall.

"I'd like a patent, please." she said.

"Who's calling?" said the clerk.

"[Indecipherable]."

A pause.

"Hello?"

Minutes later, the clerk had joined the throng, whose members had begun wielding signs:

HAIL, PROPHET!

FRAUD.

The clerk's sign read:

Nobody owns Og.

"Og" meant different things to different people. Most defined Og as the being who had invented the people of Lüz. Others insisted that the people of Lüz had invented Og. Everyone agreed on the relevant verb.

There was no consensus, within the former group, about why Og had invented Lüz. Some declared that his mirror had broken. One claimed that he had been trying to impress a woman, until the rest reminded him that in the beginning there was just Og.

(The first woman, incidentally, was whittled by Og out of someone's femur.)

The reason that Og had invented the people of Lüz was, of course, that he was lonely. That they were lonely was the reason that the people of Lüz had invented Og.

The brass knocker on the astronomer's door had, by now, broken loose. Fingers had scrabbled her windows pale. Her petunias were indistinguishable from weeds.

The astronomer contemplated her escape. With faces blockading every entrance to her home, she decided instead on fear.

“I AM ON FIRE,” she shouted through her second story window.

When this elicited only cheers, she ducked her head inside and hurried toward the kitchen. She snatched a pot from the stove and dumped the contents—boiled eggs, now cool—into the sink. Hastily she filled the pot with tap water and hauled it back to the sill. She steadied her breathing, and readied for the tip.

Too late, the astronomer registered another face. A boy had scrambled up the trellis, hoisted himself over the sill. He knelt on the carpet, breathing in knots.

“What—” the astronomer began.

“I knew about the Braille,” the boy interrupted. “I’ve known for months.”

2

According to many believers, Og had set the first pair of beings loose in a garden called "Need." To need was the one thing that the beings never had to do in the garden, which explained why they never had to speak.

When Og grew tired of watching the beings frolic in silence, he invented Law, which was Need disguised. "Don't smell the lilacs," he admonished, knowing that to say so would be to rouse in each the opposite command.

Not everyone considered Og worthy of praise. Some denied his existence altogether.

"There is pain," said the non-believers. "Therefore, there is no Og."

To this the believers cited cases of joy.

"If Og is as you say, He would banish pain," the non-believers replied.

"In a painless world," said the believers, "Og would never occur to us."

Within the hour, Og had made his discovery. There was one of the beings, drunk with fragrance, wheeling about Need on one foot. The other knelt by the lilacs, her face hidden in blooms. The betrayal was exactly as he'd hoped, but he found himself at a loss. Shyly he combed the branches with wind, gently at first, to announce himself.

The beings froze.

"What have you done?"

"Nothing," they said. It was their first word, and their first lie.

The wind tightened. To the beings, the landscape was newly decipherable, as if fed through a prism. For the first time, they could make out where they ended and the world began. Inlets appeared between themselves and other objects. Ocean, sky, and trees—once entwined—fell apart. The more they spoke, the more the change intensified.

According to the theologians of Lüz, it became appropriate then to call the beings "human."

In Year 3, a group of psychologists proposed that every conception of Og was true, in its own way.

"The existence of Og is not refutable," they announced. "Nor does it lend itself to proof. It is only reasonable to conclude, therefore, that Og both does and does not exist."

To their surprise, both factions responded. A convention was called, hosted by the lexicographers. At issue was the entry titled "Og, n." in the National Dictionary, whose first edition appeared in Year 1.

"If Og's existence is both true and false," said the non-believers, "then contradictions are true."

The psychologists nodded emphatically.

"And if contradictions are true," said the believers, "then they are also false. Your own proposal, then, we may declare both true and false."

"Well, when you put it that—" the psychologists began.

"There's no way around it," the non-believers interrupted. "You've been trounced."

"All we wanted was to put an end to your bickering," muttered the psychologists. "Carry on, then."

They gathered their belongings. Too abashed to raise their eyes, none of them noticed the change in the air. Each faction, meanwhile, eyed the other with new solidarity.

After the lie, Og retreated—whether out of boredom or rage, no one knew. Most mistook his absence for their own eviction. "We doomed ourselves," they declared, "and Og knew it."

A few suspected that Og hadn't banished the beings from Need, but from their memories thereof. The garden remained, eclipsed by words. Something had gone, the beings knew, but what it was they couldn't say. Need was intelligible, and therefore out of sight.

They renamed it "Lüz."

3

“I’m sorry,” the boy was repeating, more softly now. Evening had fallen, and with it the voices below. The astronomer watched the last picketers amble from the lawn, muttering, the clerk among them. By late afternoon the reverent few had soured, coaxed by their peers into the safety of doubt.

The boy was still crouching on the rug, his back to the window. The mug beside him had long stopped breathing. In vain the astronomer had ordered him out, then softened at the frenzy in his eyes. She’d brought him tea and orange rind, only to find him pressed against the wall, ears locked between his knees.

“I’m sorry,” he continued.

“What for?”

“I’m sorry,” he said again, as if in prayer.

Had the astronomer pressed him further, broadened her gaze from his shoulders to his hands, she might have waited out his tears. She turned instead to the kitchen, set a pan of milk to steam, and listened for his chanting to resume. Silence. When she returned, armed now with a telephone and a plate of macaroons, the room was empty.

“Hello?” she called.

No answer. The room—pregnant, still, with remembered noise—disclosed nothing. There were the picture frames, and the scenes within. There were the snow gloves on the banister, so old they had memorized her hands.

"Are you there?" she said, her voice sharp. She drew a breath to call again when her gaze snagged on an object. It was several shades lighter than the carpet, thin, and just north of rectangular. Glancing around, she knelt and reached toward it. An envelope. Manila, with no address. She flipped it over. The arms of the metal clasp lay flat. One corner of the flap had torn loose, exposing a triangle of white. Gently the astronomer pinched the clasp and, glancing once more toward the doorway, shook the contents to the rug.

Lenses tumbled out. Pages followed, a dozen sheets bound messily with thread. On the first, a title:

Final Portfolio

By [unintelligible]

The astronomer turned the page.

CONSEQUENCES OF LOSING UMBRELLA

Wind: air
chasing its tail.

She turned another:

CONSEQUENCES OF BELIEVING
THAT THE UNIVERSE IS DEAF

Og is a pail of words
that some child tipped.

"It started with the dreams."

The astronomer wheeled around. The boy was standing in the doorway, running his thumb along a ridge in the wood. Hastily the astronomer gathered the fallen lenses, shoving the pages back into the envelope.

"Night after night," the boy continued, addressing the floor. "They weren't nightmares, exactly. No falling or failing to run or anything of that sort. Just a feeling of something pressing in on me, huge and illegible."

His gaze wandered a few meters on, over the carpet. He held it still just shy of the astronomer.

"The feeling hung around me all day, like a bad smell. I couldn't shake it. I tried writing about it—writing poems. That usually helps. And writing is what I do, what I am—" He was speaking faster now, the color rising in his cheeks. "But suddenly I had nothing to say. The page was empty. There was nothing in it, nothing to find. And the feeling—writing only made it worse."

For one brave instant the boy wrenched his gaze from the floor to the astronomer's face. She was watching him steadily.

"Who are you?" she said.

With a sigh of frustration and shame the boy turned his back to the room. He was wearing a uniform, navy blue, a school crest sewn onto his shoulder bag.

"I shouldn't have bothered you to begin with," he said quietly. "It's all so humiliating. Plagiarism, that's what it is. And now, with the news all over the papers…" He cleared his throat. "It's over. I'll be found out."

"What are you talking about?"

"Please," the boy continued, turning back. "I'm sorry to trouble you like this." He reached for the envelope. "I'll just take that and go."

The astronomer hesitated. "Does this—your writing, here, these poems—do they have something to do with the Braille?"

For the first time, the boy's face relaxed. "Yes. That's the point."

"What do you mean?" said the astronomer with exasperation. "You said you knew about it. That you'd known already. What do your poems have to do with anything?"

The boy was looking past her, toward the deepening blue, where a line of gulls—drawing together, warily, like salt underground—was no longer visible.

"They're not my poems," he said. "They're Og's."

4

In the months following their eviction, the beings replaced their home with a system of signs. They crushed ants into ink and blackened the trees with illustrations of Need. What began as hieroglyphs broke apart into geometric shapes, to which the beings applied the term "letters." In time the shapes disbanded into angles and lines, as a body simplifies into bone.

(The third being of Lüz was born through a wound in his mother. He found a fourth with a wound of her own, took her name, and spent his life trying to dive back in, only to plant new versions of himself.)

Meanwhile, Og returned to populate Lüz with a series of events. Each was built of a series of facts, as a sentence is of constituent words. To the grammar between facts and events the beings assigned the term "time."

Each fact, in turn, was home to a set of ideas, and each idea to sets of things. To each thing Og assigned a function:

EYES	to rain
ICE	to cauterize
LIGHT	to bruise

[etc.]

On the last he paused:

HUMAN to signify

As a consequence of the beings' eviction from Need, the latter function could only be approximated. Ineluctable and impossible to fulfill, it led its charges in circles around whatever ache of loss or love they set out to convey. A paradoxical function, theologians agreed, thwarted by the very signs that enabled its pursuit.

For this reason, the people of Lüz reserved their most meaningful locutions for those that negated language altogether. Such locutions included "indescribable pain," "unspeakable loss," and "unutterable joy."

During periods of national mourning, speech gave way to moments of silence. A few turned the dodging of words into a practice, to which the people of Lüz assigned the term "art."

The insufficiency of signs produced in Lüz a new species of grief. The inability to voice suffering became a suffering all its own, more anonymous, less communicable, than the ache that set it off. That this more palpable grief was insoluble was never discussed.

In time, the lexicographers of Lüz codified Og's assignments in the National Dictionary. Related entries included:

Knowledge, n. Guilt.
To be, v. To owe.

The entry titled "Og, n." underwent near-perpetual revision, beginning in Year 2 with its reclassification from noun to verb. New iterations effaced the old, until the entry itself was no longer legible. In Year 12, the lexicographers scrapped the palimpsest and began again:

Og, v. To save Lüz.

Within a week, they had revised it:

Og, v. ~~To save Lüz~~. To retard its fall.

5

"Every night I would sketch constellations."

They were sipping tea. A fly patrolled the macaroons, now ossified.

"I'd wait till my sisters went to bed," the boy continued, "then climb out onto the roof. It was like sitting at the bottom of the ocean. All those gallons of air between me and the figures. My favorites were Pavo and Orion. And Cetus—the whale." He dropped a cube of sugar in his tea, inhaled.

"On one particular night, a few weeks back, my sisters wouldn't stop arguing. The younger one had asked my mother what would happen if a person were to jump into a hole that ran straight through the earth. The older one cut in to say that the question was silly because he'd melt on the way down. The first said it didn't matter, that the point was hypothetical. She thought he'd change direction—fall out the other side and then back in. That he'd continue on that way indefinitely. The older one would have none of it. He would keep falling, she said, into the sky.

"The next thing I knew I was lying on my quilt, fully dressed. The house was quiet. It was almost dawn. I didn't feel like sleeping again or washing up, so I climbed outside." He dipped a macaroon in his tea, gave it a careful bite, then set it down. "Everything had changed. None of the figures were in place. They'd all shifted, or been blotted out. Cetus was nowhere in sight."

"You know why, don't you?" the astronomer said after a pause.

"We were turning, of course," the boy nodded. "I remembered that in a moment—we'd turned toward different stars. And instead of sketching, I just sat there looking up at all that riotous motion I couldn't see, knowing that the stars themselves were long dead or plunging apart at incalculable speed." He was sitting on his hands. They were bitten raw, the astronomer had noticed. Every so often a thumb would appear at his lips, recalcitrant, for him to banish again under his thighs.

"One of the constellations looked exactly like an old logogram we studied in history, from Anatolia, a few centuries before Year 1. It was shaped like a cross, only wider, with longer arms. It meant 'negation.'"

"Logograms?" said the astronomer.

"They're like hieroglyphs," the boy replied. "Usually pictures. Signs that stand for other signs."

"So you found one. And then?"

"Light was spreading. Before I knew it night had given way." Noiselessly he dipped his spoon into his tea, stirred counterclockwise, then removed it. "I started thinking about Anatolia, about the logograms. Something in me cooled. I thought, what if they aren't just pictures? What if all this time I've been mapping what I should have *read*?"

He laughed ruefully. "And all the while it was as if I'd opened a book and seen only squiggles and lines—copied them out and called them 'rain,' as if they meant nothing beyond whatever natural thing they evoked."

"You're quite precocious, you know," said the astronomer, spooning cream into her tea. The white billowed, resolved itself.

The boy pressed on. "I tried connecting the dots into letters, but found only gibberish. Besides, how was I to know which language to pick? What I needed was an alphabet of dots. Which I had, of course. It was so obvious I couldn't see it."

He ran his heel over a stain in the rug. "I slept, woke up. Morning rolled into noon. A day later I came to my senses, found a Braille dictionary, and spent the week transcribing everything I could."

"And the dreams?"

"Right." He hesitated. "They were part of why I spent so many nights on the roof. I didn't want to sleep." The fly, which they had batted away, had returned, rounding the cream in somnolent loops. "Our portfolios were due at school, and all I had were these transcriptions. It's shameful, just—"

"I'll have another look, if you don't mind," the astronomer interrupted, reaching for the envelope.

The boy obliged. "The strangest part," he said, "is that they're nothing like the messages you found—at least, nothing like the ones they published in the Gazette. They're sort of arcane, really. More like riddles than poems."

"What were the lenses for?" The astronomer asked, flipping through the pages.

"I'd use them now and then for the really distant words. They're weak, but thick enough to sharpen a letter or two."

The astronomer had paused on one of the final pages.

CONSEQUENCES OF THINKING
ABOUT THINKING

Language, between errands,
catches sight of itself.

"That was one of the first I found," the boy said. He rose and wandered toward the window. For several minutes they remained that way, without speaking, she bent over the pages, he looking out into the gathering dark.

"What I don't understand," he said finally, "is why Og would speak like that."

"How do you mean?"

"In poems."

"What's so puzzling about poems?"

"Well, your transcriptions make much more sense."

"You think so?"

"Of course." He was growing impatient. The astronomer was still flipping through the pamphlet, chin propped on her hand. A drop of cream had moored the fly to the table's edge. "Why would Og exist at all if not to tell us what to do?"

6

Days before the release of the National Dictionary, the lexicographers of Lüz hosted a televised debate. Under dispute was the entry titled:

Word, n.

The first group demanded that the entry read "map." The second insisted on "candle."

Advocates of the former contended that words mirrored the world.

"Language is to Lüz," they maintained, "As Man is to Og."

The second group disagreed. "Words don't map the world. They make it visible," they declared, forgetting that a flame, once lit, destroys its host.

The lexicographers titled the Dictionary, *HOUSE OF THOUGHT*. Full of windows, it was, they agreed. No doors.

After the Dictionary's release, November stayed. The people of Lüz waited up for weeks. They stamped on the lakes until the ice wheezed, and grew branches. They cut the days from their calendars and flung each across the snow, until the ground was a chessboard gone mad. They wrote to May, the alchemist, but still November listened in silence, and in silence turned the rain to glass.

When at last their ink froze, they understood that there was nothing more to say. So they slept, and in the morning found the first wound in the ice.

Before the thawing of the ink and the thinning of the glass, they discovered that May had written back. They never opened the letter—perhaps out of suspicion, or perhaps because they needed to protect their belief in an elsewhere, beyond words, which could do everything but mean.

7

"So by your lights, Og's purpose is to issue commands."

The boy nodded. "That's what I've read, in any case."

The astronomer had refilled the teapot. Steam curled through the china spout.

"And before Og, there was nothing."

"Right."

"What, then, do you suppose there was to set him to the task?"

"Well." The boy took a breath. "Nothing, I know. But that's beside the point. If Og didn't issue commands, there'd be no such thing as morality. Talk of right and wrong would be just that—talk."

"Og's commands," said the astronomer. "Are they justified?"

"Of course."

"Let me put it another way. Are Og's commands inherently good, or are they good because Og says so?"

"The former, I guess. Otherwise Og would be a tyrant."

"A tyrant?"

"Well, he'd choose the good by fiat."

"Without appealing to reason, you mean?"

"Yes. To some prior standard."

The boy avoided her eyes.

"So there was something after all," she said.

"What?"

"Before Og."

"Well—" The boy's thumb found his lips. "Not exactly. No *thing*."

"A thought?"

"A standard."

"Talk of right and wrong, then. It isn't talk of Og."

"I don't—" He bit his thumb once more, and then trapped it in his other hand. "I'm not sure how we ended up here. Perhaps we've been talking in circles."

"Never mind," said the astronomer. "More tea?"

The boy nodded his thanks. They sat for some minutes in silence, listening to the evening traffic. Wind leaned against the panes, hummed its blind melody.

"There must *be* an Og, after all," the boy said finally. "You think so, don't you?"

"I don't know."

"What do you mean, you don't know?"

"Just that. Can't say there is. Can't say there isn't."

"But doesn't it bother you, the question?"

"Not especially."

"Well, it should." He lifted his steaming cup, winced, and set it down.

"Why?"

"If there weren't, Lüz would have no cause."

"And?"

"The whole world would be one great paradox. A book without an author."

"A paradox, indeed."

"How can you just—"

"What's so troubling?"

The wind throbbed on, shuttling light into the darkening room.

"You know what all this talk reminds me of?" the astronomer said, reaching for the pamphlet.

"What."

"One of your poems."

"My transcriptions, you mean?"

She had flipped to a page near the back. "This one, here."

CONSEQUENCES OF REASON

Quarrel of light and shade.

"Oh, that," the boy said, smiling faintly. "I never understood it."

"These transcriptions," the astronomer began. "They're really odd."

"I know." He reddened. "I told you, I don't know what to make of them."

"You read the title, and you expect an injunction. And instead you find a metaphor—or something oblique."

They were quiet.

"It's almost as if—"

"What do you think came first," the boy interrupted, "thoughts or things?" The question seemed to take him by surprise. He drew in his ankles, rested his chin on his knees.

"What do you mean?"

"Sorry—I was just thinking back to what you said before. About Og, and right and wrong, and all that."

"That's all right. It's just—I don't quite know what you're getting at. It's as if you'd asked me which season came first."

"Which season?"

"Yes."

"Spring, of course. Don't you think?"

"Why do you say so?"

"You have to be born to die."

"Surely that's not up for dispute." She tucked a hair behind her ear and rose, turning toward the window. Outside, the moon had just begun to hatch.

8

The fifth season struck every other year. Autumn fell, and then wind. Ropes of it, lashing the trees until the boughs had no choice but to release their hands. Warily the people of Lüz would point their faces toward the sky. A few would lean against the thickening air, let the dust into their mouths. The rest would fill their bathtubs with flour. A splash of water, then; a cup of oil. Children to swim the powder into dough.

Within the hour they would have pressed the dough into every keyhole and faucet, every knot in the floor. No seam went unsealed. Even the chimneys, corked by evening. By then the notes would have begun. Shrill at first, sending the squirrels in loops around the mailboxes, tails switching.

In Year 3, a major triad had blasted through the mouth of a rose. For one triumphant hour, the chord wove itself across the avenues, over the hills, down the throats of bees. Drunk with sound, the people of Lüz had swung open their doors. Not until they'd undressed their homes entirely did the other notes begin—out of the clovers, and then the weeds. Soon the meadows were awake, each blade howling in its separate key.

Hastily the people of Lüz would cram their houses shut, tear open their pillows and drape their clothes across the eaves, soaking up whatever noise they could. One or two would hack a crevasse in the floor. Armed with jars, they would climb inside and bottle the last few quarts of silence.

The people of Lüz sold the jars in sets of three, toward the season's end. Lobbies formed demanding the regulation of silence—the allocation of jars to minors, pregnant citizens, and citizens suffering from age. When the government complied, prices soared. A few clerks began siphoning the silence from jars into soda cans and empty vials, until the managers caught on and chased them out.

When they were lucky, the season ebbed before the looting began. The noise would thin, the air stiffen. Silence fell in time with the frost. First the orchids, then the grass—their voices softening from a roar to a shapeless whine, until the first chord was again decipherable.

The people of Lüz knew winter had come not by the quiet—to which, temporarily, they were already deaf—but by the birds. Ravens, mostly, their flocks knotting the clouds. Rain followed, and then snow, chasing the music north.

9

"It's getting late," said the astronomer. "Won't your parents miss you?" They had moved to the living room. Vases lined the mantle, flanked by shells. On the windowsill, matryoshka dolls beamed and pouted.

"I said I'd gone to a friend's for the night," the boy said vaguely. He was scanning the bookshelves, running his knuckle along the spines. Now and then he paused on a title, jostled it out, and flipped to the end.

"Still, I'm not sure—"

"You like poetry?" he interrupted, holding up a book.

"I'd forgotten about that one," the astronomer replied. She reached for it, and he handed it over.

I AM THE DOOR, it read.

"A strange little book," the astronomer was saying, "A novel in verse, as I recall. About a cartographer who sets out to draw the perfect map."

"Of the world?"

The astronomer nodded. "To-scale, no errors. When that proves too daunting, he narrows his lens to his continent, then his city, and finally his own front lawn." She was thumbing through the middle section. "He makes it halfway through the first dandelion."

"And then he dies?"

"I hope not," she said, closing the book. "I hate it when books end that way."

"Why?"

"Death belongs off the page."

The boy had wandered toward the windowsill. Nearby, a motor snarled and retreated, tossing bands of light across the far wall.

"The same goes for talk about 'the end of time.' As if, outside of time, there could be an 'after.'"

"I'm not sure what you mean."

She gave a bright sigh. "Enough of these heavy words. You must be hungry, yes?"

"No, thanks," said the boy, his voice muffled. He was kneeling just beneath the sill, a stack of papers before him.

"Did you write this?"

"That? Oh—" She was there in a moment, sliding the document gently from his hands. "That's just an old manuscript."

"You write?"

Already she had shelved it out of reach, behind an atlas. "Here and there," she was saying, "Not too often, anymore."

"What sort of writing?"

"All sorts. Mostly fiction."

"Was that a novel? Your manuscript?"

"Not really. Part argument, part myth."

"What about?"

"It's too early to say, honestly. I'm still piecing it together." She switched on a lamp. The boy was still kneeling, his back to the wall.

"I didn't realize you wrote."

"Well, there you have it."

"Any poems?" A matryoshka doll, misaligned, caught his eye. He plucked it from the sill and gave it a careful twist.

"Not exactly. For a while I wrote page-long stories. A few were only several sentences long." The astronomer had resumed her place on the couch, legs folded beneath her. "There was one— Well, I won't bore you."

"Go on, please."

"They were all a little like your transcriptions. Barely comprehensible." She cleared her throat, swallowed. "One took place in a courtroom. A trial was underway, for some petty crime. The defense was claiming insanity, and prosecution wasn't buying it. The defendant had a whole speech prepared—madness is hard to feign, you know, harder than sanity—but when he took the stand he cut himself off. He started speaking, and then seized up with his mouth half open, eyes fixed ahead, on the courtroom clock. The hour hand had begun to move. Not clockwise or counterclockwise, but away from the numerals, perpendicular to the wall. The minute hand followed, until both hands of the clock were pointing directly at him."

"And then?"

"I don't remember. There was a verdict, I think, but it didn't find its way in."

"It's funny the way you tell it," said the boy, after a pause. "As if you're recounting an event."

The astronomer smiled. "Event and invention. There's a difference, no?"

"Of course there is. There must be."

10

Both annual holidays in Lüz were marked by a variety of practices, including—respectively—the roasting of birds and the ritual domestication of trees.

The latter holiday occurred midway through the fourth season. The people of Lüz would furnish their living rooms with a single pine, anchor the trunk to a water tin and lace the boughs with ribbons and bulbs. The former ushered in the third season, sealing off the warm months with a feast. Every household in Lüz would assemble a tray of gourds and a basted swan, stuffing its ribs with cubes of bread. In advance of the meal they each offered a sentence or two—citing in their collective thanks the bonds of blood to which they owed their unhappiness.

Before the pine tree the people of Lüz would rehearse the past. Such rehearsals took the form of operettas—chronicling, in turn, each alleged incarnation of Og. The first took place in Year 0, when a woman—finding herself unconsensually inseminated—was obliged to give birth in the company of goats.

All but several documents recounting Og's second incarnation were destroyed shortly after their inception.

Most ministers denied the incarnation as such, locking the legible documents in the basements of cathedrals. The few available details depicted a figure whose opinions harmonized, more or less, with those proclaimed by the first of Og's incarnations. Rumor had it that the figure—of unknown gender and race—was born at sea, and spent a year in continuous laughter.

11

"That story of yours," said the boy, "it reminds me of an argument I overheard one afternoon, between my sisters. They'd been playing on the beach, and discovered a pattern in the sand. A trail of corrugations, they said, leading from the sea to a boulder. After a few tries they rolled it over and found a sand dollar in the socket beneath, half buried, packed with salt. They decided it had gone there to die."

The astronomer was still sitting on the couch, listening, hands interlocked. A soft rain had loosened the air.

"Much to my parents' chagrin, they brought it home. They wanted to build another, they said. To make the corpse into a blueprint for the next."

"An industrious pair."

"Well they never got going, anyhow, because they couldn't agree on where to begin. The younger one insisted on dissection. The way to know a thing was to break it up, she said. The older one refused. What mattered were the ratios, she said, the configuration of parts. Not the pieces but the whole they composed."

"Who won?"

"The older." The boy was still sitting by the sill, cross-legged, his back to the night. "By intimidation, I think. At first she said nothing. Then she held up her wrist. 'What time is it?' she asked. She was pointing at her watch. 'Eleven,' said the other. 'How do you know?' she said. 'Don't be stupid, look at the hour hand,' 'Not according to you,' and so on." He stretched his arms over his head, sighed, and let them fall.

"The younger one was just about fuming, at that point. The older one bided her time and then said, 'According to you, the second hand is more accurate.'"

"What do you think she meant by that?"

"That's what I wondered. She just repeated, simply, 'The way to know a thing is to break it up.'"

"Argument by analogy."

"I guess you could say that. It set them off again, in any case, into another quarrel. And last I checked the sand dollar was lost."

They were quiet. The rain continued, indifferent, scattering applause across the roof and the yard below.

"As a matter of fact," the astronomer began, rising to her feet, "I've got an old story somewhere that makes a similar claim."

"Philosophy?"

"Fiction."

The boy looked on as the astronomer scanned the shelves. "Strange to think of fiction making a 'claim.'"

"Why is that?"

"Stories aren't facts."

"They're certainly easy to refute," said the astronomer, her voice muffled. She lifted a vase from a high shelf, set it down, and rummaged in its wake.

"Well, that's not what I meant," said the boy. "The soundest facts are refutable, after all. You're the scientist. You—"

"Here it is," the astronomer interrupted. She was dusting off the cover of a journal, vermillion, ribbon slack along its spine. "I wrote it years ago. About a logician and his daughter."

"What happens?"

"My early years, disguised," the astronomer replied, flipping it open and letting the pages tick from her thumb. "I couldn't stand to read it through again. But there's a portion near the end, here, if I can find it."

The boy had wandered toward the vase, which was filled with branches. Gently he slid them out, one by one, and laid them parallel.

"Here—I've got it. The last few paragraphs." She ran a finger down the page. "It's his daughter's birthday. She loves the sea. He decides to build her a wave."

"A wave?"

"Yes. He rents an old sloop and makes for the horizon. Which recedes, of course, as he advances."

"Not too bright for a logician."

The astronomer smiled. "He's trying to find the origin, as it were. The source of the waves. That way he'll know where to begin."

"He gets lost, I take it."

"Not as soon as you'd think. He keeps on until evening, and then chooses a wave at random. He drops a pail in and—"

"To catch it?" the boy interrupted. He had assembled the branches—four olive, five evergreen—into a row.

"Presumably. If he can't map its cause, he thinks, he'll map its constitution. Measure the space from crest to trough, and so forth." She cleared her throat. "He drags the pail alongside the hull, in time with the wave. But he's drawn backward, of course, in the attempt. So he chooses another and scoops up the crest, only to watch it barrel on, intact."

"So he gives up?"

"Soon enough. He finds his way back home and hauls the pail into his office. Weighs it. Records the water depth. Plugs the numbers into some old equations. He works all night, until he realizes that the numbers have changed."

"Evaporation."

"Exactly. When he opens his eyes it's almost noon, the day is spilling in and the water's blasting light. His daughter is blinking up at him, papers strewn about her. He's never let her into his office before—no good reason, he thinks—but now he leads her out by the wrist. She keeps pointing at the papers, asking what they say. They're just sentences, he replies, sentences of logic. She wants to know what logic is. He tells her it's like a story, with rules." The astronomer paused, flipped a page over and back. "I'd forgotten it ends this way."

"How?"

"With a question. His daughter's." She handed the journal to the boy, pointing to the top.

"'A story with rules.'" he read aloud, "'What is it *about*?'"

For a moment they said nothing. Outside, the rain had swelled to an ovation.

"You like plots like these, don't you," said the boy, setting down the journal.

"What do you mean?"

"This one, and the others—when they're over, there's nowhere to stand. They just drop off, like a bad stitch."

"I suppose they do."

"Your point about making a claim, and all," he said, softening, "I just thought this one would end with a moral. A resolution, at least, of some sort."

"Did you have one in mind?"

"Not really." He had returned to the branches, spacing them evenly along the carpet's edge.

"Something like, 'every crest has its trough,' or 'you can't measure one wave without measuring the ocean.' Not as glib, but, you know."

"There's a piece in here about logic, if I remember correctly," said the astronomer. She was paging through the boy's pamphlet, head bowed.

"Never mind that one. I wouldn't—"

"Right here," she interrupted, holding it up.

CONSEQUENCES OF DEDUCTION

Space: time's
cancer.

"Yes, I know," the boy said, turning back to the carpet. "And that's just what I mean. How do you interpret a thing like that? There's no sense. All you can do is toss some notion into the lines, then restate it as if you've made a grand discovery."

"What's the alternative?"

"Lines that instruct. Justify. Resolve. That testify to life as it is." He took up a branch and traced a jagged loop around his knee. "And don't tell me that my transcriptions already do. Life isn't a scramble of images."

"Certainly not."

"You, especially," he said, his voice quickening. "Lines like that should bother you. Your whole career presupposes that the world is more than we make it out to be." He set the branch down and faced her. "You understand the problem, don't you? Our transcriptions don't match. I've falsified your data, or you've falsified mine. Either way, something's wrong."

"Wrong?" The astronomer was looking past him, through the narrowing rain, toward the slurred headlights beyond.

"Of course," said the boy. "Og doesn't speak in contradictions."

12

Despite widespread reports of felt separateness, isolation, and synonyms thereof, the people of Lüz shared a word: "I."

To resolve the apparent contradiction, one logician proposed to banish the word and replace it with the use of proper names.

So alien was this proposal to the people of Lüz that they phoned the politicians, who banned its passage in law. The lexicographers codified the law in the National Dictionary.

Reports of separateness persisted nonetheless. To ease the symptoms, the people of Lüz enshrined particular nouns.

Such nouns included, but were not limited to:

EMPATHY
COMPASSION
UNDERSTANDING

To redeem himself, the logician embarked on a Proof of Compassion:

Let Compassion = C

At a loss, he shifted his sights from the proof to its logical implications:

If C, then your pain is mine.

He checked the sentence for errors and, finding none, continued:

(1) If C, then your pain is mine.
(2) If I am not you,
then your pain is not mine.
(3) Therefore, if C, I am you.

So preposterous was this conclusion that the logician discarded his pen. He tried a pencil, a new page. No use.

The logician faced two possibilities: accept the conclusion, or consider it a proof against deduction.

He chose the latter.

13

"It's time I showed you something."

The astronomer was sifting through a drawer several paces from the couch. Outside the rain had dwindled, the lamps gone mute. Only wind remained to conjugate the night.

"My older sister would kill for one of these," the boy said absently, wandering toward the mantle. "She always has her eyes out for a breed called 'Clanculus.' Red and barbed, she says. With a helix. Like this." He lifted a shell from the mantle's lip and weighed it in his hands.

"Clanculus puniceus," the astronomer nodded, glancing over her shoulder. "A rare find."

"This is it?"

"That's the one."

"No kidding." He drew his knuckle across the edge of the shell, cocked his head, and ran his thumb down its glossy throat. "She'll never believe me. Such a know-it-all. Last June I found her a conch on the shore, all in bloom, half-strangled in kelp, thong weed, what have you. I rinsed it off and hauled it inside. There she was, her back to me, bent over a plate. My shadow must have given me away, because when I clamped my arm over her eyes she just kept chewing. I told her I'd harnessed the sea, that I had the proof right there. She ignored me until I swept back her hair and held the thing to her ear."

"Quite the brother."

"I know," he blushed, setting the shell back on the mantle. "But the truth is, she started to laugh. 'You're still in the thick of it,' she said. 'The thick of what?' I replied. She just laughed again and rearranged her bangs. At that point I'd retreated, conch intact, and aimed myself at some pressing task on the opposite counter. 'The great joke,' she said finally. 'What joke?' I said. That set her off again."

"Laughing?"

"Yes. My ears were roasting at that point. When I made to leave, she flung out her arms and said, with vicious delight, '*It's* listening to *you*.'"

"The conch, that is."

"Your guess is as good as mine."

The astronomer had closed the drawer. She was studying the boy from the bureau. "Did you really remember all that? All those details."

"More or less." He turned to the wall, his neck flushed. "You color in what you can."

"That line of your sister's," said the astronomer, straightening. "It's right out of a piece I wrote, months ago."

"One of your page-long stories?"

"Right. About a religious scholar. She sets about reinterpreting the 'fall of man.'"

"The eviction from Need, you mean?"

"In a sense. But she claims there was no eviction. At least, no flight from one region to the next. What was meant by the 'fall,' she thinks, is instead a kind of reversal. An inversion of sight. Man wasn't banished, she says, just doomed to see things in reverse."

"What do you mean?"

"That to see things as they are, you'd have to hold a mirror up to time."

"What would you see?"

"All sorts of things."

The boy had resumed his place at the mantle. He ran his thumb under the wooden lip, examined it, then blew. A cloud of dust appeared, its fragile orbit tangling the air.

"Rain ascending, for instance. Sand congealing into rock." She pointed at the fireplace. "Those ashes would assemble into newspaper, old letters, logs. Contraction would replace expansion, order entropy."

"What about the fall of man?"

"That's the point."

"No, I mean, would the 'fall of man' become the 'man's flight,' or something?"

"I hadn't thought of that."

"Well," the boy said, turning toward her. "It sounds awfully optimistic to me."

"How so?"

He shrugged. "Nothing would be lost."

"I don't know about that." The astronomer adjusted her arms, and he could see that she was holding something pale. She shifted her forearm again. It was a notebook, bound in wire.

"Is that it?" He said, brightening. "That, there, in your arms. You said you had something to show me?"

14

In Year 16, the lexicographers of Lüz set out to winnow language down to a word. The Great Excision, they called it.

"RELINQUISH ALL SYNONYMS," read the announcement in the Daily Gazette, "i.e. MARRIED SENTENCES, CLAUSES AND NOUNS."

Within a week, half a dozen pairs had arrived, scrawled in the joints of envelopes. The author would strike out the phrase he wished to obliterate, leaving its partner intact:

(1) what will have been
~~(2) what is~~

The lexicographers sifted through the remaining five. The last pair read:

(1) I love your qualities.
~~(2) I love you.~~

"Veto," came a voice.

The lexicographers turned as one. It was the postman. He stood in the corner of the meeting room, lips pale.

"What was that?" a lexicographer asked.

"Never mind," replied the postman, hastening to the door.

"Wait a moment," the lexicographer said. "Perhaps you're right."

"Impossible," said another. "You are your qualities, are you not?"

"Indeed," said the first, "but aren't you more? Your memories, for instance. Surely those—"

"Revise the sentence, then," the second persisted, "tack on whatever you'd like. 'Memories,' 'history,' 'fears.' Let's get on with it."

The first considered, then nodded. A rustling followed. Moments later, sentence (2) was excised.

"They weren't synonyms," the postman said quietly.

"They must have been," said the first lexicographer. "If a difference exists, then when I love 'you,' I love something else."

"Something else," the postman nodded, "without a name."

15

"I don't understand," the boy was saying. They were seated on the windowsill, a spray of documents between them. Night slanted through the glass, dense as loam.

The astronomer was watching him evenly, legs crossed. The wire-bound notebook lay prostrate in her lap.

"There must be some mistake," the boy continued. He seized the page before him and brought it to his face. "I mean, I'm sure you double-checked and all, but this can't be right."

"What makes you say that?"

"Just look at it." He snapped the page around and pointed.

"2 + 0 = 3"

"It's nonsense," he went on, his eyes hard. "You might as well have discovered a reptile with fur. Worse than that. A shape with only two sides, or a square with five."

"I'm not sure I follow."

"You can't take this seriously. If you do, you've got yourself in a bind, don't you see?" He brandished the page. "These numbers negate the foundations of arithmetic. You've pitted the empirical against the a priori, the very axioms beyond which—"

"Now, now, don't get ahead of yourself."

"I don't think you understand."

The astronomer took a breath. "When a child is born, does arithmetic collapse?"

"What are you talking about?"

"One and one become three, don't they?"

"That's—" he burst out. "That's trivial. That's beside the point." His thumbnail appeared at his lips, and he bit it furiously.

"That example you gave," the astronomer continued, glancing politely to the left. "About geometry. The impossible shapes. I heard love defined that way once. As a figure with only two sides." She chuckled. "You're quite imaginative, really. When I—"

"Please."

"I'm sorry?"

"This is serious."

A silence descended, sharpened the edges of objects. At length the boy swung his heels to the floor and returned to the mantle, where he busied himself with a matryoshka doll.

"It's an absurdity, is what it is," he said at last. "It has to be a fluke."

The astronomer said nothing.

"How could it not be?" he continued. "It's a contradiction in terms. If you really did double-check, and the transcription is right, then you might as well have proven that the sky isn't speaking at all."

"Have a look at this," the astronomer said gently.

The boy faced her, doll in hand. She was holding a sheet of paper to the light.

"You are innocent."

The boy studied the image. Then, he seized the page and flipped it over.

"You are to blame."

His face darkened. "You found another, you're saying."

"Another what?"

"Contradiction."

"You could call it that."

The boy turned away from her. In the window she watched him set his lips into a dam for imminent tears. "It's as if you'd opened a sack of dice to find a jumble of white cubes, empty of dots," he said finally. His voice had thinned, and seemed to issue from the rug. In the silence he brought the matryoshka doll to his chest, rested his chin on its painted head. He took a long breath, and glanced once more at the page. It was then that he spun round.

"These images are the same."

"The photographs, you mean?"

"Yes—of the sky. You've used identical images."

The astronomer was quiet.

"And that sentence of math," he continued, eyes wild.

"The false equation—where is it?"

She produced it.

"This one, too!" he exclaimed. "The photographs are identical. They match."

"So it seems."

"Well, then." The boy's face—undone by incredulity—reassembled into obstinate relief. "There *must* be an error. A flaw in your transcriptions."

"You think so?"

"Easy to correct, no doubt," he replied, generously. And then, into the astronomer's silence, "You see what I mean, don't you? The same image can't yield opposing claims." He gave a short laugh. "It's the same data, after all. The same text."

16

Several weeks into the Great Excision, a logician presented the lexicographers with a new discovery. A contradiction, he reported, had infected the following verb:

Regret

"Suppose I regret action X," he began. "If X precipitates my regret thereof, then to wish away X is to wish away my own regret."

The logician cleared his throat. A bulge appeared west of his brows, where his temple met his hair.

"One cannot regret, therefore, without refuting oneself. The verb is logically impossible. It has no place in our Dictionary."

He loosened his jaw, and continued.

"The confusion runs much deeper, actually. All talk of remorse is a symptom, see, of the mistaken belief in counterfactuals."

"Counterfactuals?"

"In an 'otherwise,' so to speak. A 'might-have-been.' Speech regarding such a realm is nonsensical—no better than flexing a phantom limb."

"We'll do everything we can," one lexicographer cut in, patting the brick of paper before her. "We've got your case right here, top of the stack. For now, I'm afraid we'll have to move along."

Nodding his thanks, the logician turned to go. Outside, evening had narrowed the autumn light. The air was brittle, the ground spangled with frost. Hastily the logician gathered his coat about his shoulders, tucked his chin. It was a long way home, but he would manage. Eyes low, he set out over the starry earth to wherever it was he would have to be.

Concomitant with the Great Excision was a project undertaken by a band of renegades, who occupied—in secret, one autumn noon—the public library. They gagged the librarians, cleared the shelves, and carted the books to the National Sieve. Into the Sieve they fed page after page. They began with Philosophy, whose distillation yielded the following questions:

(1) Why is the world?
(2) Why are we?

What distinguished the philosophers from the poets of Lüz was the assumption that questions (1) and (2) were distinct.

17

"That was my father's," said the astronomer. "An ancient thing. I'd forgotten I left it there."

The boy had retreated to the bookshelves. He leaned now against the atlases, fingering a pipe.

"Calabash, with a porcelain bowl," she continued. "Worth a fortune, no doubt."

Numbly the boy brought the mouthpiece to his lips. On the windowsill, new transcriptions lay strewn about, framing the old. The images were barely decipherable now, the constellations eclipsed by pen marks.

"As soon as the sun cleared the pines he would be at it, puffing away, till the whole house smelled of camphor. One day I asked him where he'd put the sound."

"The sound?"

"I had mistaken the pipe for a flute. I was barely four, at the time. He never corrected me. Strange—considering his infatuation with accuracy. He was a logician, by trade, ever obsessed with policing language, mending its wounds, inoculating syntax against any and all ambiguity. Anyhow, he told me he was playing it backwards. Swallowing the music and spitting out its ghost."

A sheet of paper nodded off the sill. Before the astronomer could move it had pitched away from her, hewing the air in its lateral descent.

"One afternoon he left it on the porch, still lit. I pressed my lips to the mouthpiece and gulped. Nothing happened. I must have inhaled accidentally, because the next moment I was coughing myself inside out." She cleared her throat. "After that, music never sounded the same. It had an undertow. Every melody seemed to mask something else, some excluded core. It was better for it, I thought—the music. More beautiful, more dangerous."

The boy shot a listless glance in her direction. "You don't have to amuse me, you know." He set down the pipe. "There's nothing left to say."

The astronomer met his gaze, unblinking.

"What I don't understand," he continued, "is why you published the Braille in the first place. It was cruel, really. You knew all along."

"Knew what?"

"That it was all a farce!" His voice tightened. "That the messages depend on your angle of sight, or on whatever crop of stars you happen to map. That you can read in whatever you like."

"It's because it's saying everything, then. The sky. That's why you're upset?"

"If it's saying everything, it's saying nothing."

The boy held his mouth ajar, breathing lightly. He seemed newly aware of his lips. Only after a tremor caught his chin did he clamp them shut.

"In that case, you didn't plagiarize," said the astronomer.

"What?"

"Your transcriptions. They're yours. You read them in."

"Oh, those." Surprise rinsed his face. "It doesn't matter, now."

"Why not?"

He ran an anxious finger across his upper lip, as if applying balm. "What matters is the sky. That it's mute."

"We just transcribed a whole paragraph."

"Yes, but we could have decoded something different, utterly different, using the same dots. If anything goes, then the sky is an alphabet, nothing more."

The astronomer was straightening the documents, sliding them back into the drawer.

"And don't tell me the contradictions you found are reconcilable," said the boy, gathering himself. "They're contradictions. They cancel out."

"There's no hope of clarity, now," he went on. "I don't see how you can redeem the project, if that's what you're after.

You might as well set out to build a tree with sheets of paper."

Above them, a shingle broke loose and fell in brisk arpeggio down the roof. The astronomer was gripping the sides of the bureau, head bowed.

"Have you ever seen a rose window?"

"What?"

"A circle of glass with stone lattice—"

"I know what it is," he interrupted. "And yes, though I can't remember when. Why?"

"You should stand before one in the morning, facing east. You'll be blinded, nearly. Chromatic uproar. The whole spectrum."

"What are you getting at?"

"Nothing in particular. Just a memory."

The boy shifted his weight. He was still standing in the shadows, arms akimbo. "You're trying to draw an analogy, aren't you."

"How do you mean?"

"With the colors, and all. 'The whole spectrum.' It's quaint."

The astronomer listened in silence.

"The window and the sky. The color beams and the conflicting messages."

Still, she said nothing. A low moan sounded outside, far off, the lament of some distant machine.

"I'm sorry to inform you," the boy continued, "that you've gotten nowhere. The colors conflict, all right. They're incommensurable. Divided by *stone*."

A parabola of hair slid from the astronomer's barrette. She blew it back, noiselessly.

"I don't see why you won't admit it. We've spent our time transcribing nonsense. Better to face the error than—"

"The colors," the astronomer broke in. "They cancel out, you're saying."

The boy hesitated.

"Red and cyan," she continued. "Blue and yellow. Black and white."

"They don't *cancel out*. They're opposed, chromatically. Like the messages." He straightened. "The point is, your analogy works against you."

"And if they can't be reconciled, the messages, we might as well quit deciphering them."

"Yes, exactly. If the same text is yielding contradictions, there's no underlying sense."

She had turned toward him, arms folded, new patience in her voice. "The rose window, then—it's a kind of proof."

"A proof?"

"The rose window, at dawn."

"What are you saying?"

"A host of chromatic contradictions."

"And?"

"From which, as you see it, we can draw a conclusion."

"What conclusion?" he demanded.

"The nonexistence of light."

18

For the third time in as many years, a logician alerted the lexicographers to a troubling discovery. The news arrived in a telegram:

DESIST IMMEDIATELY STOP
GREAT EXCISION A HAZARD STOP
SYNONYMS REQUISITE STOP
CUT ONE CUT ALL STOP

Mystified, the lexicographers summoned her in.

"What's happened?" they asked.

"If my calculations hold," she began, "synonymy is more than marriage. It's relation by blood."

"You've lost me," a lexicographer replied.

The logician handed him an index card. On its face was a string of words:

JOY   delirium frenzy agitation   PAIN

"According to our Thesaurus," she said, "the second word, 'delirium,' is synonymous with 'joy.' The former is a synonym of 'frenzy,' which is synonymous, in turn, with 'agitation.'"

The lexicographers nodded expectantly.

"Which leads us, regrettably, to 'pain.'"

They said nothing.

"As you'll note," the logician concluded, "'pain' contradicts our inaugural term."

"Perhaps the case is unique," said one lexicographer, after a pause.

"I'm afraid not," she said, and presented a second card:

COURAGE nerve apprehension FEAR

The lexicographers shifted uneasily.

"Another exception, perhaps," one suggested.

Unabashed, the logician produced a third card:

BLACK ashen WHITE

She was reaching for another card when a lexicographer cut in. "So they're cousins, then, the antonyms. In that case, what do you propose?"

"As the examples imply," said the logician, squaring her shoulders, "synonyms are walls. Remove them, and terms collapse into their opposites."

There was a shuffling.

"A difficult balance," she continued. "Bound to give way if the Excision proceeds."

A murmur had risen among the lexicographers.

"Haven't you…" one began, clearing his throat. "Haven't you proven the reverse?"

"I'm sorry?"

"There's a problem, all right. The kinship of antonyms. But, this business of sustaining walls…"

"That's the trouble," another broke in. "There are no walls, is what you've shown."

"I don't understand."

"Our Dictionary," he continued. "It's built of doors."

19

"You still haven't answered my question," the boy said quietly. He was kneeling before the fireplace, poker in hand, prodding the scabbed logs deeper into their nest of ash.

"What's that?" the astronomer replied. She had settled in an armchair, a glass of ice water balanced in her lap. The boy's glass—which she'd placed on the bureau—remained untouched.

"You know. Why you published the Braille."

"That would take a while, I'm afraid."

"I don't mind."

"You'd really like to know?"

"Yes."

She took a long sip, then set her glass on the floor. "Do you remember the slew of articles in the Gazette last year, about the Grand Model?"

"That discovery in physics, you mean?"

"Right. Of the equations that link the two leading physical theories, formerly considered incompatible."

"How could I not." He jabbed at a log. "My sisters nearly had a fit. They'd been rooting for the Model ever since it became suddenly plausible."

The log, soft with remembered heat, relinquished its form to the surrounding coal.

"Implausibly enough, I had a hand in the project. I'd gone to school for astronomy years ago, after abandoning fiction."

"Writing it, you mean?"

She nodded, drawing her legs beneath her. "I wanted to discover, not invent. *This* world was infinitely grander, more finely wrought, than any I could conceive. Nobler, I thought, to try to fathom it—in some small way—than to conjure up my own."

The boy's expression had thawed to one of equable attention. He stood now, returning the poker to its wooden claw.

"They were dizzying at first, the courses. Like thinking in a new octave. I buried myself in the lab, wrote a credible thesis, and scored a research appointment at a university of some repute. With a lot of luck and modest effort, I found myself on the coattails of the team behind the Model—a junior position, peripheral at best. By then, though, a certain ambivalence had begun to pollute my mental life."

"Ambivalence?'"

"Disillusionment, to put it simply. Cerebral nausea. The creeping certainty that I'd mistaken the whole enterprise for something it wasn't."

"What do you mean?"

The astronomer reached for her glass. "That I'd tried, naïvely, to wrestle the scientific endeavor into a sphere it didn't occupy."

The boy frowned, edging toward the bureau. In the window, the refracted moon looked heavier. Its iron glow fell with new severity across the avenue, arming the trees for dawn.

"As I saw it," the astronomer continued, "the sciences promised to codify the natural world—or rather, to document its grammar. To make it legible. To make it speak. To make matter *mean,* as it were." She glanced away from the boy, who had lifted the glass of water to his lips. "Gradually my confusion came to light. There was no final cause, no achievable end. Instead, progress unfolded by negation. Tenable theories were refutable, scientific only insofar as they invited contrary evidence. The repudiation of one model summoned in the next, and so on." She chuckled. "Self-flagellation, you could call it. Writ large."

A spot of water appeared on the rug, near the boy's toe. He obscured it with his foot.

"The shape of the earth is a perfect example. Thought to be flat, as you know, and then round. The disproof of the latter view, of course, ushered in the most recent shift from a round to a toroidal model. Adopted once the geophysicists factored time into their calculations."

The boy nodded vaguely. "Self-flagellation," he began. "I know what you mean, but it's an odd way to put it."

"In my dim understanding, at least, there was no *goal* to the enterprise, no reachable axis against which to measure our advance. Instead, the possibility of error was the criterion of truth. That was the beauty of the method, and its limit. It had no fixed horizon."

The boy had drained his glass. He wiped a pearl of moisture from the base, then set it back on the bureau. "What about the Grand Model? That was their goal, wasn't it?"

She nodded slowly. "Did you read about what happened next, in the weeks following the discovery?"

He shook his head, then reconsidered. "A little bit. They called in the cryptographers, didn't they?"

"They did. There were the requisite tests, of course. They're still not finished—they'll never be—recalibrating, revising, running the numbers through their various sieves. Meanwhile, though, the directors of my team found themselves at a loss. They'd arrived at their purported aim—synthesized our models into one indomitable set—and had no idea how to proceed."

"So they tried to decode them," said the boy, suddenly alive, "the equations. As they would a language."

"Exactly."

"The headline—what was it?" he continued, running his fingers through his hair, "something to do with Og, as I remember."

"Right," the astronomer replied. "Wait here."

She returned a moment later with a copy of December's Gazette. The headline shouted:

OG'S COLOPHON

"What's that, again, a 'colophon'?"

"A publisher's emblem, printed nowadays on the spine or title page of a book. It used to serve as the closing inscription—offer a few details about the book's authorship and production."

"So the world is a book, is what they meant."

"Obliquely. That ascent to metaphor was a symptom of a mounting hubris, I'm afraid."

"How so?""

"Well, as you put it, there was nothing left to do—as they saw it—but to treat their equations as a new and foreign language. To decode them."

"Have they gotten anywhere?"

"Not far. But they've managed to leach significant funds from a few gullible sources."

"And you don't think…" the boy broke off, watching her from the bureau.

"It was an oversight, a gesture beyond the purview of science. Poignant, in a way, but when it comes to promulgating—"

"*That's* why," he cut in, his eyes bright.

"I'm sorry?"

"Why you published the Braille. It was a parody. A caricature. An implicit critique."

The astronomer was quiet.

"Well?"

She eyed him warmly. "Argument by analogy. That's your forte, isn't it? In any event, I plan to withdraw from the project this week. No doubt I'll be fired anyway, for temporarily usurping the news."

The boy blinked, gathering himself. "A little underhanded, if you ask me. But—" He toed the rug with his foot. "So you really think they're mistaken? With the decryption, I mean?"

"They are, if they believe that it's science they're doing," she replied, exhaling. "It's not as if the impulse is unfamiliar to me. I was the one lamenting their failure to breach the semantic domain, to favor the why over the how, et cetera. But what they're after..." She hesitated, cleared her throat. "It's more like fiction."

"What is?"

"Their quest to make numbers signify—to invoke something *else*, so to speak. To do with symbols what Og did with dust."

20

A month after the crisis of synonyms, the lexicographers of Lüz faced a new calamity. So grave was the report that a logician delivered it by hand.

"Our Dictionary speaks in circles," the logician announced, handing the lexicographers an envelope.

"Circles?" they said.

The logician nodded. "Concentric circles. *HOUSE OF THOUGHT* has no speakable foundation."

"As you'll find," she continued, "every noun in the sample contains in its entry another noun, whose own entry contains another, and so on."

"What's the trouble?" a lexicographer asked.

"Consider the term 'knife,'" sad the logician, shifting her weight. "A 'cutting instrument,' according to our Dictionary. An 'instrument' it defines as a 'device,' which it defines, in turn, as a 'thing.'"

"And?"

"The definition of 'thing' is 'object.'" She paused. "And the definition of 'object' is 'thing.'"

The lexicographers were quiet.

"There's the trouble," she went on. "Nearly every noun traces back to 'thing,' whose definition loops back on itself."

"'Nearly,' you said?" a lexicographer began.

"Yes," said another. "What about natural objects? 'Snow,' for instance. Surely that's immune."

"You'll find that one in the envelope, coincidentally," the logician replied.

"Well, what of it?"

"The entry for 'snow' reads 'water vapor,' and the entry for 'vapor' reads 'substance.' Leaving us, unfortunately, in the same coil."

"How so?"

"The definition of 'substance' is 'material,' whose definition, in turn, is 'substance.'"

The lexicographers eyed one another.

"Mounting evidence suggests that the problem is not unique to nouns," the logician continued. "Most verbs, for instance, trace back to the term 'activity,' which traces back to 'state.' The entry for 'state' reads 'condition,' whose entry reads..." She coughed politely. "'state.'"

"Well, then. What do you suggest?" said a lexicographer.

"If I were you, I'd scrap the revision," she said.

"Of the whole Dictionary? That isn't—"

"The problem runs too deep," she went on, lowering her eyes. "There's no hope, now, of renovation."

"Surely you can't mean…" said one lexicographer, raising his voice.

"You have no choice, I'm afraid, but to begin again."

21

"Have they decoded anything at all?" said the boy. "The cryptographers, I mean, from the Grand Model."

He had completed a slow circle round the room, dragging his thumb along a seam in the wallpaper. He stood now against the doorframe, one socked heel propped against the hinge.

"Only nonsense, as you'd imagine," the astronomer replied. "The last I heard a debate had broken out among the cryptographers. One faction is claiming that the equations express a question. Another, a command. Still another insists that they're declarative sentences—purely descriptive." She took up her glass and tipped the last thread of water from the base.

"One group," she continued, "not commissioned by the team and still unknown, as I take it, to the general public, has adopted an angle that infuriates the rest. They hold that the Model embodies all three. Question, command, declaration. That the set of equations is stating one word."

"Which?"

"'I.'"

An object on the wall had snared the boy's attention. It was a cane, mounted on a platinum hook. He reached toward it.

"If you wouldn't mind," the astronomer said gently, raising a palm.

"Oh," the boy stumbled. His hand—inches from the cane—redeemed itself with a new errand.

"I'm sorry to startle you. It's fragile, is all. An antique. Beechwood shaft. Never in use, as far as I know."

"An heirloom?"

"Not quite. A colleague of my father's had it restored for him after he lost his leg."

"Why didn't he use it?"

"Never had the chance. He was bedridden indefinitely, after the operation. For a while he worked from home. He'd undertaken a project with the lexicographers, and a few of them would drop by now and then, with their cordial nods and black umbrellas. They were wrapping up the third edition of the Dictionary, and had hired him and several others to help refine the latest draft." She blinked, glanced toward the ceiling. "Not that he shared any of this with me. He was maddeningly private, always, about his work. Whenever I asked about it he'd just wink and deliver some unrelated fact."

"Like what?"

"A whole medley, each one stranger than the next. 'Ants bury their dead,' for instance. 'Helium can't freeze.' 'Every morning finds you miles away from where you fell asleep, relative to the sun.'" She laughed. "I'd be seething at that point. So I'd interrogate each one."

"Each fact, you mean?"

"Right. I'd ask him 'why,' on and on, until the explanations dropped off."

"How do you mean?"

"The line about helium, for instance. When I asked him why it couldn't freeze, he mentioned something about its atomic structure. Then conceded that freezing might be possible, under drastic pressure. Sooner or later he'd have no information left to cite. 'That's how it is,' he'd say, or 'I don't know.'"

"And then what?"

"Well, that's how I felt. I couldn't fathom how he could stand to live in a world whose every fact, no matter how plain, lacked a substructure. Whose chains of explanations bottomed out. The whole project of knowing seemed to me no less absurd, I told him, than trying to build a floorless room."

A sudden darkness had appeared outside the windowpane—winged, head ticking.

"He would wink again," she went on, "soberly, this time, and tell me I was on to it."

"On to what?" said the boy, eyeing the pane.

"Some theory of his, which he'd proceed to explain. Most of them were facetious, I'm sure, though they bewitched me at the time."

"What sorts of theories?"

She considered. "That the world was an enthymeme. That one was his favorite."

"What?"

"An enthymeme—an argument with a hidden premise."

"I don't understand."

"Well as he put it, the world followed from a set of axioms—including, for instance, the law of noncontradiction—one of which was missing. That missing axiom was the source of all confusion. To find it would be to see the world as it is: the conclusion of a perfectly sound, deductive argument."

"So you could know it just by thinking?"

"Precisely. The difference between thoughts and things would collapse."

The boy was edging toward the pane, tilting his chin for a better view of the bird.

"How would you go about finding it?" he asked. "The hidden premise."

"That was the trouble, of course. To find it you'd have to know something about it."

"How come?"

"Otherwise, you wouldn't know where to start."

With a muted cry the bird abandoned the sill, veering off toward the neighboring roofs.

"In any case," the astronomer continued, "I'd question him endlessly, just as you're doing, until he'd sigh and say he had it in his drawer."

"The hidden premise?"

She nodded. "I snuck in, of course, the first chance I had. The air was denser than I'd expected—that afternoon's pipe smoke, sifting fontanels of light out of the general gloom—and I had to pull my collar up over my mouth. His desk was massive. Maple wood, a dozen drawers. The first one I tried was locked, and in the next I found only notes. Symbols scattered here and there, cordoned off arbitrarily by coffee rings."

"Venn diagrams, you mean?"

"That's right." She smiled. "An accidental order."

"So you didn't find it?"

"As an afterthought I checked what I thought was his pencil drawer. At first all I saw were a few scraps of paper. Paragraphs in some ancient tongue." She ran a hand over her hair, exhaled. "An odd hobby of his, that was—translating books into dead languages."

"What sorts of books?"

"History, mostly. Said it intensified the reading experience—made discovery into design, as he put it."

"So the premise wasn't there?" said the boy. "In the drawer, I mean."

"After a moment I realized that the sheet of paper was obscuring something else, like a canopy. And then—I couldn't believe it. There it was, my eraser collection. I'd lost it days before, and hadn't finished a drawing since. They were neon, shaped like animals. Owls, lions, fish. Two of each."

"Just piled up, you mean, under the paper?"

"No. That was the strangest part. They were standing upright in two parallel lines, each one facing its partner."

The boy swallowed. "So there was no premise?"

"Not that I could see. I would have rummaged around some more, but when I looked up he was standing in the doorway."

"I thought he was bedridden."

"Not yet."

"Was he angry?"

"He ordered me out with what must have been mock alarm, though it terrified me at the time. I sidled off, ashamed, and never asked him about the animals."

"What—" the boy began, tipping his head to one side. "What about the Grand Model?"

"What do you mean?"

"Isn't that a kind of answer? Not a premise, I guess, but a solution."

"According to the scientists. But by the lights of his 'theory,' the world was *solved* already. The point was to chase its presupposition—the axiom, as he put it, from which everything followed."

"Og, you mean?" said the boy, with an affable frown.

"You could call it that, I suppose."

"So," he continued, brightening, "What does he think of the Model?"

"He's not around to appraise it, I'm afraid," said the astronomer. "Though I'm sure he'd make his opinion known."

"Oh, I'm sorry. I didn't mean—"

"Don't worry, it's been decades already. The cruelest part isn't the death, anyhow."

"It's not?"

She shook her head, lightly. "It's all there is that's left to say."

22

In Year 12, the people of Lüz resolved to measure time not by its passage, but by its accretion in rings. They maimed their clocks and set out for the capital, where the viceroys had assembled ninety shovels. Within days the viceroys had dug a pit a mile deep. Into the pit they scattered hour hands and the seed of an evergreen. A year passed unrecorded, while the seed dreamed in roots its eventual boughs.

With only minute hands to live by, the people of Lüz agreed on collective acceleration. Seconds dilated into minutes, minutes into hours. One day unfolded into ten. In the capital, the viceroys tipped jarfuls of milk into the pit. Underground, the roots had mummified the hour hands, pointing them skyward.

"All's accumulation," the viceroys murmured, refilling their jars. At last, near evening, a tongue of green parted the soil. Hastily the people of Lüz uncapped their clocks and spun the minute hands to a blur. The trunk appeared soon after, coursing through the soil toward the chimneys above.

By then the axe was ready, sharpened so deftly that the edge was no longer visible. The crowd grew quiet. One viceroy dug his heels into the soil, lifted the axe over his head, and swung it with a cry into the thickening trunk. Measurements were taken, alterations assessed. Surgeons jimmied the blade until the edge was flush with the core:

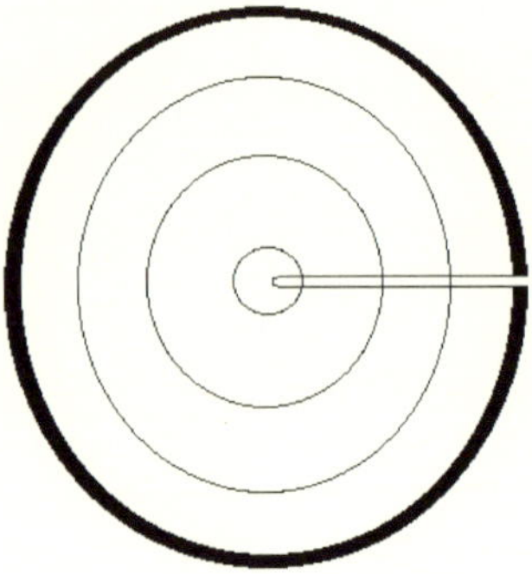

Moments later the blacksmiths arrived, armed with steel, to lengthen the blade as the rings multiplied.

"Time's radius," declared the viceroys, "is the length of this blade."

The crowd applauded.

"Suppose," said one blacksmith, "we'd like to calculate the hour at hand?"

The other blacksmiths smiled apologetically.

"A valid question," said one viceroy, "it's no trouble. Allow me." She bent her head, scribbled something on her palm, and held it up for the crowd to see:

$$Now = (2)(\pi)(r)$$

"The evergreen is our clock," the viceroy announced. "To calculate the hour, recall the equation above. Plug in the length of the blade, and you'll find the tree's circumference."

She glanced at the blacksmith, who was nodding already. "The circumference is now."

That time was not a feature of the inanimate world was discovered in Year 13 by the optometrists of Lüz, who deduced as much from the following image:

Looked at once, the image depicted a hare. Looked at twice, a duck. Despite their apparent synchrony, the simultaneous recognition of both hare and duck was impossible. The eye imposed a sequence where none prevailed.

From this result the optometrists inferred that Lüz was just such an image, dismembered by her people into "then" and "now."

23

"That lone group of cryptographers," said the boy, "the ones provoking the rest with their decryption of the Model, its single word—" he broke off, smiling faintly. He had settled on the couch, his toes buried in the cleft between two pillows.

"What about it?" the astronomer replied. She was listening from the armchair, winding the chain of a lamp around her forefinger.

"Nothing, just—it explains a lot. My sisters had been following the story, as I mentioned. Last week the younger one was suspended from school. She'd stood up during algebra, out of the blue, and announced, 'Og is 'nothing.'"

"Doesn't seem to merit suspension."

"It didn't, at first. But the next day she said it again."

"That Og was nothing?"

"No *thing*. That's how she pronounced it, at least according to her account later that evening. Predictably, she'd been instructed to stand in the hall. She complied, only to burst back in with another declaration." He gave an exasperated laugh. "More like a sermon, actually."

"What did she say?"

"'You're all symptoms,' she told them, 'symptoms of Og. In light of this, I am sorry to report three facts.' Silence ensued, as you'd imagine. Then she went on. 'First, that you all testify to the same disease. Second, that there is no known cure. Third, that the disease will remain as invisible to you as it would to a fever and chill and swollen throat, too estranged in character and kind to sensibly infer a common source.'"

The astronomer looked on, bemused. "The cure is death, presumably."

"I don't think she meant as much," said the boy, glancing away. "She wasn't trying to be wry. She's horribly earnest, generally. Nothing like our older sister."

"The collector of shells?"

He nodded, exhaling. "The younger one—she's been dragging around all week, after the episode at school. Yesterday she buried herself in her journal. Hardly noticed when my older sister plowed in waving the Gazette, with your transcriptions on the cover."

The astronomer had switched on the lamp. A pentagon of beveled glass hung nearby, unbraiding the light.

"I snuck a look, yesterday afternoon."

"Where?"

"In her journal," the boy said solemnly. "It was rotten, I know. I couldn't resist." A patch of color—indigo knit fuzzily to red—traversed his neck. "She's always suffered an aimless kind of grief. Pockets open up in her days. 'Nowhere time,' she calls them. Once in a while I come home to find her lying on the floor, immobile, letting her gaze climb across familiar objects." He laid his cheek on the arm of the couch. "In her journal there were no complete sentences."

"What were there?"

"Well—" he sighed again. "Just a list, ordered by date. And a title. *Almanac of Pains.*"

"Pains?"

"I only remember a few. There were at least a hundred, stretching back to last year. 'Pain of calendars' was one. 'Pain of snow.'"

The patch of color hesitated, resumed its course over his jaw.

"'Pain of leaving something unsaid,'" he went on, "'Pain of saying it. Pain of asking, 'Am I happy?'"

The astronomer listened in silence. The wind had intensified, breathing a syntax into the predawn hush.

"I don't mean to make her sound self-pitying," he said hastily. "It's the opposite, really. She's always beating herself up about something or other. Apologizing. Confessing thoughts. Taking pleasure in her own undoing. When they cut her suspension short she seemed almost disappointed."

"Do you think that's why she acted out?"

"Probably. She needed…" he began. "Well, she needed a crime, I guess."

"What for?"

"To populate her guilt."

24

On an autumn morning in Year 49, the people of Lüz awoke to find Memory reversed. Recollections of the day to come wafted into their conversations, their morning jokes. History loomed, swept of images. The future, meanwhile, fell into view.

Few sensed the difference at first, except to notice—privately and with vague discomfort—that thought had taken on a new flavor. Until they glanced at the date on the morning paper, most mistook tomorrow for the day before—the latter seeming, respectively, ever more remote.

As noon approached, the change intensified. Regret pivoted into apprehension, disappointment into dread. Quarrels erupted over wrongs not yet inflicted. Familiar objects stupefied their beholders, worn as they were with evidence of prior use.

For over a week, elation struck. Economists declared an end to uncertainty. Strangers, yet to marry, sought each other out. The young looked with awe at their skin, familiar now with the striations still to come. For the dying, the world was fresh—stripped clean of losses and spoiled hopes, innocent of irreparable wrongs.

As if in retrospect, future events assumed a new logic. Generals shifted their sights from weapon construction to the etiology of impending wars. Recessions were newly intelligible, droughts circumvented. Accident was transmuted into law.

If the Great Forgetting, as it came to be known, had ended more quickly—before concluding as it did, at last, in Year 51—the people of Lüz might have remembered it more fondly. That initial week might have seemed a consolation, a proof that their ambitions weren't entirely vain, that there was something after all for which to wait. They might have longed to reinstate the Forgetting, done their best to blot out the past that reappeared one December morning, as if it had never gone. They might have missed what they'd seen of the future, had it not been for a strange affliction that set in shortly after that first, ecstatic week. For months no one spoke of it, and when they did it was reluctantly, with something like shame.

The first signs emerged a few weeks after Memory's reversal, when teachers of grammar found themselves confronting widespread confusion about the subjunctive case. "What do you mean, *were to be*?" the children asked. "What will be is there already." Questions multiplied about another tense altogether: the future perfect. "*What will have been*," they continued, "Where is it? Where do things go, once they happen?"

The same questions haunted vocabulary lessons, where the word "nostalgia" elicited only more confusion. With nothing to remember, there should have been nothing to miss. And yet nostalgia persisted, more insidious now, less forgiving in its machinations, as—like wind changing direction—it aimed itself at the landscape to come. Gradually the people of Lüz understood the loss implicit in the children's frowns. No longer was the future—once elapsed—accessible to thought. Instead, the Now erased it. Tomorrow, for all its promises of fact, remained just north of the given hour, never arriving.

25

The astronomer had switched off the lamp. She rose now and ambled toward the window, gazing out into the lengthening mist.

"That 'nowhere time' of your sister's," she said. "It sounds familiar."

"What do you mean?"

"I did my share of lying on floors. During my months in research, especially. Ennui overtook me. I'd call it loneliness, if I were braver. My life became an alibi for the one I could have lived. The forbidden otherwise, so to speak."

"What sort of life?"

"A permutation of my own, as I saw it. The version of recovered chances, preempted mistakes, articulated loves. The life in which I was my own author—thoroughly, not halfway."

"In any case," she continued, "I performed my usual habits convincingly enough. Eventually I found myself buying used books just to read the annotations of strangers."

"Did you find anything worthwhile?"

She considered. "A few weeks ago—shortly after my team called in the cryptographers—I picked up a slim paperback, tangled with notes. Philosophy, I think it was. On the last page was scrawled, in capitals, 'THE PROBLEM IS THAT WE THINK THERE IS A SOLUTION.'"

The boy narrowed his eyes. He had begun blinking more frequently, staving off sleep.

"At the time, I took it as affirmation of a looming resentment toward my line of work, which—as opinion will—was aiming its florescent bulb at all the indifferent particulars of my life, blanching them just enough that I might infer their unanimous applause."

"So you published the Braille."

"I did. And you were right in your remark, earlier. It *was* underhanded. Justified, maybe, but uncritical. Driven by fear."

"Fear of what?"

"Of having misread my own desire, forfeited the life I'd set out for, initially."

"The writing life, you mean?"

The astronomer was still facing the window. Dawn embossed the branches, revived by the wind.

"It wasn't too late," she said. "I'm out of practice, but that's no matter. The pages are opening back up." She softened. "I finally understand, in any case, that I predicated my career on a false dichotomy."

"What's that?"

"Invention versus discovery."

"Discoveries are inventions, you mean?"

"The other way around."

The boy's lids had fallen. He shook himself, rubbed his eyes. "Invention… How do you mean?"

"Well, I don't write *fiction*, anymore, in the usual sense."

"What do you write, then?"

She hesitated. "I'm not sure how to put it. I suppose I try to balance the real with the possible. What is with what might be, or what might have been."

"Aren't they opposed? Facts and counterfactuals?"

"You'd think. It's hard to see, though, how we could do without the latter—the 'might-have-been,' the 'possible,' whatever you want to call that domain. Regret, for instance, would be nonsense. As would gratitude, anger, relief."

"Why?"

"Each one draws its meaning from an otherwise, no? Or rather, from the fact that things could have proceeded differently."

"Hmm," the boy murmured, lashes entwined.

"Anyway, I didn't mean anything fancy. Just that the more authentic my writing felt, the less it seemed my own."

"Theft," the boy said dreamily. "All writing is theft."

"What's that?"

"Some aphorism."

"Seems appropriate, given—"

"Does this have anything to do with that manuscript?" the boy interrupted, opening his eyes abruptly. "The one you were keeping by the windowsill? That you wouldn't show me?"

The astronomer folded her arms. "Somewhat, yes. It's a work in progress. Thought experiments, mostly. Variations on the actual. All a symptom of the same relentless impulse that coaxed me into astronomy."

"What kind of impulse?"

"To find, I suppose."

"Find what?"

She was quiet. "In any case, my hope is to weave real events into the manuscript—polished, maybe, but with a grounding in fact."

"Who's in it?"

"I don't know yet. More than one person, certainly. Whoever they are, I'll probably omit their names."

"Why?"

"To make them habitable."

"And the events?"

"There's the rub." She took a breath. "Conversations, probably. Exhumations. There's one particular memory that I've considered putting in a character's mouth." She gave a soft laugh. "The trouble is I've replayed it so often that it's been sanded down, lost its edges. Taken on a fabulistic hue."

"What is it?" the boy asked, his voice blurred. A lock of hair fell across his forehead, nudging his eyelids shut.

"Late September," she began. "Corridor of my childhood home. Low voices are wafting through the wall, from my father's room. He's been gone for over a week. 'Getting well,' I've been told. An infection in the knee." She tucked a hair behind her ear, cleared her throat. "His door is wide open. I peek around the frame, plotting my entrance. At first all I see is the headboard, cherry oak, obscenely bright. He is laughing. The warmest sound I know, at first, hideous only once I register the sheet. Lavender, smoothed across his frame. The mound of his right leg, and the valley beside it. Boulder of hip dropping off."

The boy murmured something unintelligible.

"Amputation, I learn later. 'It hasn't worked,' the doctors are sorry to report. Instead, the infection has spread." She glanced at the boy, lowered her voice. "They drive me to the hospital, to his alabaster room. He holds my hand, repeats a sentence. I don't listen. Instead, I memorize his face. For my eventual drawing, I reason. And it's the thought of that drawing that keeps me sitting up. That leads me home in a straight line. That prevents me from asking, as I'll wish I had throughout my childhood, to take his glasses home."

A ring of white was spreading on the windowpane, parallel to her lips. "When I'm led out, they're still on his face. I think, 'if I could just put them on, just look through them—once, only—I might see it. Where he's gone. What I've been looking for, my whole impatient life. At least then,' I thought, 'I'd understand what it *was* I was after.'"

Another murmur sounded from the boy, elsewhere, a rebuke of some dreamed proposition. Outside, the sky hung low and blue and blank.

Notes

Citations of images and arguments,
in order of appearance:

1. The photograph of the night sky on pages 1, 2, 52 and 55 appeared in Volume 29 of Popular Science Monthly (New York: D. Appleton and Company, 1886). The image is in the public domain and its author is unknown. Accessed November 3, 2012. http://commons.wikipedia.org/wiki/File:PSM_V29_D082_The_night_sky_seen_through_a_telescope.jpg.

2. An allusion to Plato's Euthyphro dilemma— crudely, "is the good loved by the Gods because it is good, or is it good because it is loved by the Gods?"—appears on pages 24-25. Some, the astronomer included, conclude from the dilemma that one can posit an objective moral structure without positing the existence of God(s). Plato. *The Last Days of Socrates: Euthyphro, Apology, Crito, Phaedo* (London: Penguin Books, 2010), 10a – 11b.

3. The Anatolian logogram to which the boy alludes on page 18 indeed resembles a cross, and has been translated as "negation." The language thrived in Anatolia (modern-day Turkey) from 1400 BC to 700 BC. Yakubovich, Ilya. *Anatolian Hieroglyphs*, in The Encyclopedia of Ancient History (Blackwell Publishing, 2012). Accessed December 8, 2012. http://dx.doi.org/10.1002/9781444338386.wbeah24237.

4. Joseph Jastrow's Duck-Rabbit illusion on page 89 appeared in Volume 54 of Popular Science Monthly (New York: D. Appleton and Company, 1899). Accessed January 30, 2013. http://commons.wikimedia.org/wiki/File:Duck-Rabbit_illusion.jpg.

5. An allusion to Plato's Paradox of Inquiry—briefly, "one can't search for either what one knows or for what one does not know, since if he knows it, there is no need to search, and if he doesn't know it, he wouldn't know what to look for" —appears on page 83. Plato. The Last Days of Socrates: Euthyphro, Apology, Crito, Phaedo (London: Penguin Books, 2010), 80e.

6. I discovered the sentence "THE PROBLEM IS THAT WE THINK THERE IS A SOLUTION" (page 99) scrawled on the inside cover of a heavily annotated copy of Wittgenstein's *Tractatus Logico-Philosophicus*, courtesy of Amazon.

Acknowledgments

A version of this document was submitted as a senior thesis to the English Department of Amherst College in April 2013. Chapter 24 originally appeared under the title "The Great Forgetting" in *Fairy Tale Review* vol.10, No.1 (2014). I am grateful to Amherst's English Department for its support of the project, and to Amity Gaige, George Hagan, Norman Lock, Brian O'Connor, and Marisa Parham for their encouragement and editorial advice. Special thanks to my parents and to Daniel Hall, without whose wisdom, critical eye, and generosity of spirit this project would have remained a pattern in the ice.

About the Author

Lindsay Stern is the author of *Town of Shadows* (Scrambler Books, 2012).